For Renee, and her many small humans —E.P.

For my brother Jonathan —S.G.

Farrar Straus Giroux Books for Young Readers
175 Fifth Avenue, New York 10010

Text copyright © 2016 by Eric Pinder
Pictures copyright © 2016 by Stephanie Graegin
All rights reserved
Color separations by Embassy Graphics
Printed in China by RR Donnelley Asia Printing Solutions Ltd.,
Dongguan City, Guangdong Province
Designed by Roberta Pressel
First edition, 2016
1 3 5 7 9 10 8 6 4 2

mackids.com

Library of Congress Cataloging-in-Publication Data

Names: Pinder, Eric, 1970- author. | Graegin, Stephanie, illustrator.
Title: How to build a snow bear / Eric Pinder ; pictures by Stephanie Graegin.
Description: First edition. | New York : Farrar Straus Giroux, 2016. |
    Summary: To build the biggest and best snowman ever, Thomas enlists the
    help of his "bear" brother who would rather sleep.
Identifiers: LCCN 2015030872 | ISBN 9780374300203 (hardback)
Subjects: | CYAC: Snow—Fiction. | Snowmen—Fiction. | Brothers—Fiction. |
    Bears—Fiction. | BISAC: JUVENILE FICTION / Family / Siblings. | JUVENILE
    FICTION / Concepts / Seasons. | JUVENILE FICTION / Animals / Bears.
Classification: LCC PZ7.P63235 Hn 2016 | DDC [E]—dc23
LC record available at http://lccn.loc.gov/2015030872

Our books may be purchased in bulk for promotional, educational, or business use.
Please contact your local bookseller or the Macmillan Corporate and Premium Sales Department
at (800) 221-7945 ext. 5442 or by e-mail at MacmillanSpecialMarkets@macmillan.com.

HOW TO BUILD A
SNOW BEAR

ERIC PINDER

Pictures by
STEPHANIE GRAEGIN

Farrar Straus Giroux • New York

The day after a big blustery blizzard, snow sculptures of all shapes and sizes appeared on Thomas's street.

Thomas couldn't wait to
make a snowman of his own.

As soon as he got home from school,
he tiptoed past the snoozing bear,

found a carrot and two buttons
to make a nose and eyes,

and rushed back outside to build the
biggest and best snowman ever.

Rolling a giant snowball for
the legs was easy enough.

The middle part took more work.

Huff. Puff. Whew.

The third part proved hardest of all.

Thomas stretched and hopped, but the snowman was so tall that he couldn't quite reach high enough to put the head up top.

Wobble. Bobble. Plop.

Thomas needed a helping hand—or
a helping paw. So he went to wake
up the bear.

Bears like to hibernate on cold winter days. So when Thomas gently rocked the bed, the bear just yawned and rolled over.

Thomas noisily raised the shades to let the sun pour in.

Rustle. Bustle. Zip.

The bear opened one sleepy eye.

"Look outside!" Thomas said. He pointed at the snowman and explained how much fun playing in the snow would be.

But the bear just blinked
and fell back asleep.

Thomas tried other ways to wake
up the hibernating bear.

Turns out bears in blankets aren't
very ticklish.

If you sing to a sleeping bear, he
will bunch up his pillows like earmuffs.

If you entice a sleeping bear with your favorite toy, he will cuddle with it instead of getting up to play.

On cold winter days, bears just like to dream.

Thomas remembered that bears have a big appetite when they wake from hibernation. So he raced downstairs and made a scrumptious snack.

The aroma wafted up to the bear cave.

At last, the sleepy bear came
sniffling and shuffling downstairs.

Thump. Bump. Clump.

Thomas waited patiently while the bear chomped and chewed. You should never rush a hungry bear.

Munch. Crunch. Yum.

As soon as the bear ate the last delicious
bite of the biggest, yummiest cookie, Thomas
said, "Now we can play! You can help me finish
the snowman." He ran for the door.

Bomp. Clomp. Patter.

The bear hurried after him, carrying two
big round cookies for the snowman's ears.
"Great idea!" said Thomas.

Together they bounded outside,
their feet scrunching on the snow.

Bears are tall and good at climbing—especially
when their big brothers help lift them up. The
bear *streeetched* and plonked the snowman's
head on top, then added the nose. And the
eyes. And finally, two cookies for the ears.

Now it wasn't the biggest, best snowman
ever—it was the biggest, best *snow bear* ever!

Bears are furry and
warm, so they like to play
outside on snowy days, all
bundled up.

Thomas and the bear took turns sledding
on the little hill behind their snow bear.

Zip. Slip. Vroom.

Together they waded through the deepest drifts

to make a snow cave, too.

And when the sun slipped behind a cloud
and it was time to come back inside for
cocoa, Thomas discovered some other
things that bears like to share.

A favorite book.
A warm fire.
And best of all, a wondrous winter day
with a big brother.